MARGOT

and the

MOON LANDING

MARGOT
and the
MOON LANDING

A.C. FITZPATRICK

ERIKA MEDINA

annick press
toronto · berkeley

Annick Press Ltd.

We acknowledge the support of the Canada Council for the Arts and the Ontario Arts Council, and the participation of the Government of Canada/la participation du gouvernement du Canada for our publishing activities.

Library and Archives Canada Cataloguing in Publication
Title: Margot and the moon landing / A.C. Fitzpatrick ; Erika Medina.
Names: Fitzpatrick, A. C., 1990- author. | Medina, Erika illustrator
Description: Illustrated by Erika Medina.
Identifiers: Canadiana (print) 20190169907 | Canadiana (ebook) 20190169915 | ISBN 9781773213606
  (hardcover) | ISBN 9781773213637 (PDF) | ISBN 9781773213620 (Kindle) | ISBN 9781773213613 (HTML)
Classification: LCC PS8611.I8918 M37 2020 | DDC jC813/.6—dc23

Published in the U.S.A. by Annick Press (U.S.) Ltd.
Distributed in Canada by University of Toronto Press.
Distributed in the U.S.A. by Publishers Group West.

Printed in China

annickpress.com
Find A.C. Fitzpatrick on Twitter and Instagram: @fitzywrites
erikaim.com

Also available as an e-book. Please visit annickpress.com/ebooks for more details.

For my parents.
–A.C.F.

For Eduardo García and my dad, Angel Medina.
–E.M.

Every day and most nights, Margot read and reread her favorite books.

They were all about space travel.

Her mother tried to convince her to read different books about robots, or gorillas, or princesses.

But she soon gave up.

Margot was only interested in one thing.

Whenever Margot learned a new fact, she would share it with everyone she met.

"Did you know that the first creatures sent to space were fruit flies?" she said at dinner.

"That's nice, sweetheart," said her mother.

"Make sure to finish all your dahl and rice."

"The first men on the moon were named Neil and Buzz," she told her teacher, a little louder than usual, just to make sure she was heard.

The teacher was unimpressed.

"Please pay attention, Margot," he said.
"We are learning arithmetic right now."

During lunch break, the children went outside
to play. Margot brought her books with her.

"Do you want to join us for kickball?"
the other girls asked Margot.

"In outer space, the astronauts eat special food squeezed out of tubes,"
Margo said, holding open her book in case anybody doubted her.

But the girls didn't even look at the page.
They had already started dividing up the teams.

Late at night, Margot didn't have to think
about dinner, or math, or the schoolyard.

She could read about space until lights out.

And then read even later under the covers,
shining her blue flashlight on the pages.

Margot fell asleep wishing she never had to talk about anything other than space ever again.

When she woke up, Margot went down to the kitchen table where her mother was preparing breakfast.

"Good morning, Margot," said her mother.

That's one small step for man, one giant leap for mankind.

Margot had meant to say "good morning."

"Eat your oatmeal, dear," said her mother.

Margot tried to ask for a spoon.

Houston, Tranquility Base here.
The Eagle has landed.

It was no use, every time she opened her mouth all that came out
were transmissions from Neil Armstrong's 1969 mission to the moon!

"That's nice, sweetheart," was all her mother said.
"Hurry up or you'll be late for school."

"Margot, please answer the question on the board," said her teacher.

For once, she knew the answer. It was an easy question.

The surface is fine and powdery. I can kick it up loosely with my toe.

Surely her teacher would realize
something was wrong!

Instead he said, "Margot, please pay
attention. The answer is clearly seven."

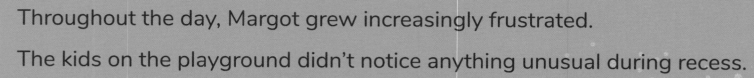

Throughout the day, Margot grew increasingly frustrated.

The kids on the playground didn't notice anything unusual during recess.

The gym teacher told Margot to pipe down.

The school nurse simply gave her a glass of water then sent her back to class.

By the end of the day, Margot felt like crying.
She went into her bedroom and slammed the door.

Margot inhaled deeply, opened her mouth, and let everything gush out:

There is a plaque on the front landing gear of this Lunar Module. First there's two hemispheres, one showing each of the two hemispheres of the Earth. Underneath it says "Here men from the planet Earth first set foot upon the Moon, July 1969, A.D.

WE CAME IN PEACE FOR ALL MANKIND!"

That did it.

Margot grabbed
a marker.

She knew she wasn't
supposed to write on
the walls, but she no
longer cared.

Writing out her feelings felt good.
She kept going.

Every word she scrawled somehow made her feel lighter.

Soon, a whole wall filled up. Margot got lost in her writing.
She forgot about the rest of the world.

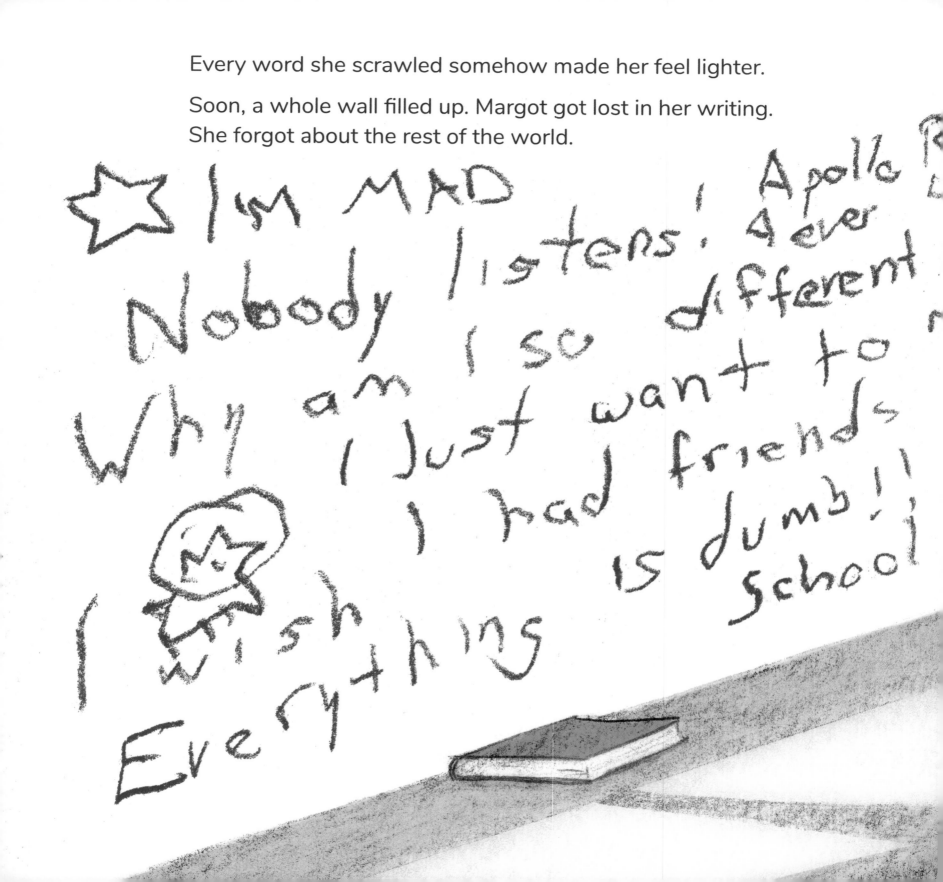

I'm
lonely
om the other kids?
d all day
I'M SAD
wish people would listen.
HATE THIS!
boring

When her mother came into the room, Margot didn't even notice.

"MARGOT!" said her mom.
"What on earth is going on in here?"

Margot waited for something to happen, but instead her mom got very quiet.

She read all the words on the wall and then read them again.

Margot started to clean the walls with the corner of her sleeve.

Her mom rested a hand on her shoulder. "I have a better idea."

Margot's mom came back from the
basement carrying bucketfuls of colorful paint.

Together, they transformed the wall into a deep galaxy blue.
They added a moon and some stars and even a rocket ship.

On the other wall, Margot's mom taped two large sheets of paper.

"The pièce de résistance," she explained.

"So you always have a place on the wall to write your thoughts."

"I'm hungry," said Margot.
"Can we have spaghetti for dinner?"

Margot wasn't sure exactly when her
voice came back, but she was glad
she had someone there to hear it.